wonderful world

stories and poems by Janie Reynolds

To Roddy

A guiding star,

Janie x

wonderful world

stories and poems
by Janie Reynolds

pardus print

Published in Great Britain in 2022 by Pardus Print, 6 Milton Crescent, Eastbourne BN21 1SP, United Kingdom.

ISBN 978-1-7397558-0-5

contents

**stories
white**

Confessions of a beached whale

Might a bird gliding through a stunning blue sky be fretting about what she said to a different bird the day before? And wondering if she ought to fly back and try to make up? Do dying animals know when they're dying? Do they call on their significant others just beforehand and whisper repentances in their ears? Trying to fill in the gaps before they drop. Or do they let the gaps just be?

Do animals even have a concept of time? Those are questions for the zoologists. All I know is that appearances can be deceptive. You don't know what's really going on in that bird's head.

When I was dying, not only did I know it but I knew exactly how much time I'd got left. And this was exactly as I had planned it. Just like that bird, you'd never have guessed the sheer sinisterness of the contents of my head as I lay there motionless on my death bed. To an uninvested passer-by I might have looked quite the picture of humility - breaths subsiding, form acquiescing, with all the grace of an autumn leaf. But, like some poor beached whale, stranded on the banks of life, systematically dehydrating under the lurid glare of the hospice lights, my thoughts, oh Lord, my thoughts, were running maniacally around my skull, like a losing football team near the end of extra time.

And my eye was on the ball – the 'ball' being the heart and oxygen monitor beside my bed that gave me all the information I needed. I can't say it wasn't nerve-wracking, knowing when I was going to die, and if I'd had the strength to lift my hands to my mouth, I'd have bitten my nails all the way to hell. But I couldn't lift them, not even to grab a pea from the trolley meals as they came, smelled of gravy and then went. I just had to lie there, wilting, half in darkness, half in the shrillness of the day, the weight of life bearing more and more heavily upon me than the weight of death. And as I did, I rehearsed over and over, the exact words I was going to mouth to the each of the critters that hung around my bed, waiting for my departure. I had the ultimate act of emotional washing up to pull off, in order to perfect the ultimate ramification-free exit.

Family life, to me, had been a life-sentence. It would be an understatement to say I was not fond of the critters who I had been lumbered with in that life: a pig of a wife, a good-for-nothing son and a village idiot of a daughter. But my wife cooked me dinner every single night and had a safe admin job at the local solicitor's which kept the wolf from the door. So, I had a choice - my days dogged with drama and sulking, insults and injuries, or, staying schtum 'til the bitter end and keeping what I really thought of the critters for my last words and dying breaths. No brainer.

To my son, Andrew, I was to say that he was a lazy, useless waste of space. That I'd never wanted him. He was a burst condom. But his mother had refused to have an abortion.

To Elaine, my wife, I wanted her to know that I'd never loved her, not even liked her. And, anyway, I'd been having an affair with Katie at number 17 for 45 years.

As for my daughter, Cherry, well, she had to know the truth. That she was never mine, she was the plumber's. But that her mum had kept it secret for her whole life out of shame. Because the plumber was more than one sandwich short of a picnic.

When, finally, I noticed the flashing lights slowing undeniably and the oxygen saturation dropping sharply, I knew it was time. But, oh, was I in for a terrible surprise. Death cannot be played, it turns out. As I tried to speak my mouth just hung open. The tissues of my tongue and the muscles of my mouth had packed up some moments before my brain. My perfectly prepared sentences just collapsed at the back of my throat and lodged there.

They wrote on the death certificate that my breathing just stopped. But that wasn't it. I choked to death on my confessions. And the critters all went home happy, damn them.

The chocolate beanstalk

One spring day, a petite girl, in a boho dress and flat leather sandals, wafted merrily along the high street. She held hands with a tall and fancy boy, who rather dwarfed her with his swanky tailored clothes, and lops of jet-black hair which fell splendiferously across his large square forehead. The pair's soft faces and airs and graces betrayed the fact that they had only just met, at a party a few weeks ago. They had quickly fallen in love, the girl having been broken-hearted by a teacher in the town and the boy by a lady chocolatier.

As they strutted along the pavement, the boy became extremely nervous. He tugged the girl quite quickly into the road, and over to the other side. He hoped she wouldn't notice, but of course she noticed. Not only was she perplexed by the impromptu change of course, but also by the beads of sweat around his temples and an unpleasant clamminess of his hand. She also saw how his eyes kept flitting across the road to a chocolate shop they had just missed. And the way he then, unnaturally, turned his face to talk to her, masking it from view.

'I thought you loved chocolate?' she asked inquisitively.

'I used to,' he replied, and then quickly changed the subject to whether she'd like to go on a summer holiday with him. She thought this was all rather peculiar, seeing as it was only October. She also found it very odd that her new boyfriend, who had talked an awful lot about all the different types of chocolate, ever since she had known him, was now denying that he even liked it.

A few months later, because new love can heal hearts, the two set off, all pink-lensed and virtuous, on an adventure to live in the countryside. They found a white-painted, rose-trellised cottage by a river, which was ruled by an old, wise willow. The tree had watched over it for centuries. Poets, musicians and artists had all once lived there, but the willow had no recollection of any of that, because he was a tree. Babies had been born in that house and people had died there, but the tree had no memories of that, either. All he knew was the feel of the winds as they circled his watery bark and the sense of the warmth or the cold of the breeze as he stood. He had forgotten the floods and darkest of winters that had frozen him stiff in the past, and the smouldering summers that had bleached and crisped his slender branches. He didn't wish for more or less rain, bigger or smaller clouds or hotter or colder sun. What purpose had such reminiscing other than to disturb his peace and quiet?

During their first summer together, the sweethearts found a perfect place, under the wispy web of the willow, to lie and read and enjoy the exotic flowers. But as winter fell, the cottage became cold and windy, and, outside, the rain pelted, the river flooded and the land muddied. The old tree sensed a deep unease from the house. And often, he would see the boy driving his car back into the town where he would visit that same chocolate shop. The boy would laugh and cuddle with the lady chocolatier. He would tell her about the coldness of the cottage and she would sympathise. Then she would give him some chocolate beans, some of which he'd scoff right there, and others with which he'd fill his pockets. Then he would drive back to the cottage and lie about where he had been.

From then on, he would help himself to a bean or two when no one was looking, because he liked the taste and was reminded of the days he used to enjoy them so often. And once his pockets were empty, he would drive back into town, to the chocolate lady, and ask for more.

What he didn't know was that there was a hole in the lining of one of his pockets. And that, as he had been lolloping around the country cottage, chocolate beans had been dropping on to the floors and into the furniture. One night when they were in bed, the young woman asked the young man if he could smell chocolate. 'I smell chocolate everywhere I go in the house!' she said. 'But I don't know if it's just me.'

'Well, I can't smell it,' said the boy. 'It must be just you.'

Some days later, when she was cleaning the house, the girl found some chocolate beans under the cushions of the sofa. She told the boy and asked if he knew where they had come from.

'No idea,' he had said. 'How strange!'

But the girl was no fool and she knew he was lying. 'You have been visiting that chocolate shop when you go into the town,' she said. And at that moment, all that was once sweet to her became bitter.

As spring came, the young man and woman still lay and read under the willow, but one after the other. One day, when it was the boy's turn, he was lazing and turning and shifting and, without his noticing, some chocolate beans slipped through his pocket onto the ground and rolled in between the gnarly roots of the willow.

When it was the girl's turn to sit there, she could not, because she found, to her horror, that slithering brown saplings were sliding up and wrapping round the great tree's roots, like pythons. And there was an overbearing smell of chocolate coming from them.

'A chocolate beanstalk!' she cried, and ran back into the cottage. But instead of finding the boy relaxing, she found him carrying a heavy suitcase to his car.

'So, you're leaving our romantic home for the unknown streets of the town?' she asked him. 'Where's your courage to be brave in a light and dark world?'

'When you speak, all I can think of is chocolate,' said the boy. 'Eighty per cent cocoa, bitter, pralines, milk, creams and vanilla.'

And then he drove away, back to the beginning of the story. But, probably with another girl next time.

Saddened, the girl returned to her beloved willow for whom she felt so sorry. She didn't care even to look down at his strangulated roots, but simply wrapped her arms around him and hugged as tight as she could. But, although the tree was grateful for her kindness, he was as fine and strong as ever. He had no fear of anything that had risen out of beans from the past, which, of course, don't exist. He had simply ignored the silly chocolate beanstalk, which only aspired to imaginings. And as the girl cuddled him fondly, she realized that the smell of chocolate had completely disappeared. So, she did look inquisitively to the ground, and was surprised to see that there was no longer anything there except the same ancient roots, as there had been for hundreds of years. It was as if no beanstalk had ever been.

And at that moment, all that was once bitter to her became sweet.

Reflection

When we were young, you and I, and the world was yours and mine. Time took such time to drag our days from dawn to night, our wide eyes learned with every blink of something new.

The allure of the heart, the enticement of the flesh, all so fragile yet so effortless. That was fifty years ago.

Now, with each and every further flourish of a day, the hours race blindly to the end, barely allowing us to catch up with their tails, before sleep beckons us back to our beds.

Today I am reflecting. That our beauty truly has been abandoned. Your old, unbuttoned chest, once bursting with delicious caramel cream, is florid now, and fussy. Speckled with pantones of pink, and café au lait spots, flaking and raised, where we have carelessly absorbed the sun throughout the many years. If I had watched you closer, lain beside you all the time, I might have caught them slowly creeping, from freckles to flat wafers, and might have slowed that metamorphosis.

If I had groomed you, more meticulously, I might have followed with my eyes, as the once abundant, glorious web of fine and golden hair, that hovered over you like fairy wings, disintegrated, allowing for the invasion of such wayward, loosely knitted skeins, and hardened threads of single, salt and pepper curls. I might have soaped the pleats and rolls of sebaceous, weary skin, at the base of your neck, where the thin, gold chain I gave you tucks away.

I look with sympathy, into your tired and tiny, dull and milky eyes. That water with the tears of age, muted by all that you have seen.

All that you have not seen. All that you will never see. Burrowed deep beneath those heavy lids, above which, eyebrows, huge brushes of bristle, wild as Prometheus, great, grey hedgehogs, shroud them.

How you worry, my love, how the furrows and folds of your frown tell of a thousand disappointments, piling heavily upon your nose.

Yet, defying all that sorrow, hang the smile lines of delight, descending to the downturned corners of your melting mouth, outlines of a cheerful life. And, at the sides of your eyes, the laughter lines, clawed indelibly into your flesh, yet still dancing.

And how I smile at that bulbous, orange-peel nose, rosaceous, so colourful and bright, spewing forth, the pores you poke and rub on me as we kiss.

I love you still, my old man, as we succumb to gravity and decay. You sleep by my side, for better, for worse and we'll sleep together forever.

Coke cans in the wind

One night, in America, I was sitting on the bed in my hotel room. I was trying to write, and I realised that, to write a book worth reading, I might have to start with a more interesting line than 'one night I was sitting on the bed in my hotel room.'

I thought deeply. 'How can I write something interesting?' I closed my eyes and waited, for words to find me, and pictures to emerge in my head. So that one would follow the other, and so on and so on, into a story.

But not much happened. 'I can't write,' I thought.

So, I hurled myself off the sumptuous bed and walked towards the large triple-glazed hotel window. As I did, I could feel footprints forming under my bare feet. At the window, I looked out over the unknown city and saw that a storm was rising.

As I stood gazing, my fingertips brushed gently against the fine silk of my pyjamas as my arms hung loosely by my sides. A pale truck sped along the empty road hauling its load like a lone camel. Empty Coke cans rattled along the pavements with the litter of tramps, lifting and spinning in the wind like juggling balls. A boy, curled over in a dark hoodie, stopped, just below my window, and hesitated for a moment before staring straight up at me. How could he have possibly known I was there?

I noticed it was deepest winter, because the rim of the boy's hair glistened with frost and his breath formed a cloud under his hood. I felt like an intruder. A spy. Was it allowed to look down on life? Was it wrong? Should I be down there talking to him, or picking up the Coke cans and placing them in waste bins?

Then I recalled I was supposed to be trying to write something interesting. I returned to my bed and started writing about how I left my sumptuous bed to walk to the window, felt the footprints beneath me, and the silk pyjamas, and the truck and the Coke cans, and the boy who knew I was there. And I smiled as I realised that, if I wanted to write, there was always a window to look out of. Yet how often did I forget that. How often was I of the opinion that I could write with my eyes shut.

Second date?

I had such a great time last night. First date. But it's 10am and he hasn't texted.

That's it then. Strange. I thought he liked me. Acted like he did. Even did that thing that's supposed to mean they do – brushed his arm across mine mid-conversation. Kissed me on the cheek at the end as well. Why hasn't he texted? I wasn't his type. Too old. Too out of shape. He wore Fat Face jeans so he must be fit.

He noticed my bingo wings. Wanted more leg. Women who succeed on blind dates are slim. They work-out and wear a skirt above the knee. Jut their bony knee caps in his direction. Wear sleeveless tops. Have visible cleavages. It's rude of him not to text me. Do all men know they're the one who's supposed to text after a first date? I'll google it. (15 minutes later.) No definitive answer. Everyone says different things. He must know I'm waiting for a text from him. It's rude. I'm getting angry. I'll ring my son.

"Matt, do all men know they are supposed to text the woman to ask for a second date?"

"Muuuum! I don't know. If you wanna text him just text him."

"But I don't like texting men. Then I'm doing the chasing and that puts them off. They need a challenge. It's in their genes."

"Well, don't text him then!"

Thanks, Matt.

He just doesn't want to see me again. Like that film, or is it a book? - "He's just not that into you." And, women never call men in films. I can't call him or text him. I just have to wait. He wouldn't have kissed me if he didn't like me. Maybe he's nervous that I don't like him. Maybe he's read a dating book that says the man mustn't text the woman for a set number of hours or they'll come across as too keen. Maybe I'd better text him. I'll make a cup of coffee then I'll text him. What shall I text? 'Had a lovely time last night. Thanks for the wine and the conservation'? Or, should I say I'd like to see him again? Otherwise he won't know I do. He might think I'm just being polite but don't want a second date. Maybe, 'Hi. Had a lovely time last night. Would you like to do it again?' But that's too much pressure. It's only the next morning. And it did say on Google not to put a question mark in a text until you're in a proper relationship. I'd better google it again. (75 minutes later) No idea whether to ask him if he'd like a second date. Everyone says different things.

It's midday and he still hasn't texted. This is stupid. I'd better just risk it and text him. What shall I write? 'Hi Tom, had a lovely time last night.' Doesn't really lead anywhere. But musn't ask a question. I should put an 'x' or it's not like dating. Or should it be a winky face? No that's slutty. Just x or xx? x. xx's too much. We only met for an hour and a half.

Right.

Send.

Sent.

(90 minutes later) Why hasn't he replied? I wasn't his type. He noticed my bingo wings. Wanted more leg. Do all men know they're the one who's supposed to text after a first date? I'll google it.

Happy ever after

You, you were 16. Tall, clever, rebellious.

Me. I was too young to fall in love. You were the handsome prince and I the enchanted princess. My love for you was virginal, like the lily-white sanitary pads I pulled from their pastel wrappers.

Young love is always played out to music. We put Rod Stewart records on the turntable and fondled to the Bay City Rollers. Our hearts beat in time with the songs we played, racing at the climax then stopping in our creamy chests until the next one started.

We drank cider to ignore our vulnerabilities and build the courage to scream 'This is me!' We smothered each other loudly and obliviously. You, my first taste of something that unfurled around me, without my having to do anything except look pretty. Everything had been predictable and planned before you. But now, it was as if you had given me a pass to a fairground ride through wonderland. As I was carried along, I waved my white-gloved hand goodbye to loneliness, a rotten self-image and my need for attention. I had found my other half. I was fifteen.

We ate popcorn and snogged through *Saturday Night Fever* then made out in the cinema car park. When I wasn't with you, I read *Jackie* magazine and *Cosmopolitan*, proud to be a new member of the club for whom they were written - girls with boyfriends. I bought copies for the tiny free perfume bottles sellotaped to the covers and tested them to see which one I thought you'd like best. I filled my head with articles like 'How to look hot for him' and did quizzes on whether you loved me and to what percentage we were compatible. I shoplifted so much '17' makeup and underwear that I got caught. I couldn't have cared less. I got to keep the cosmetics and the lingerie as no one asked me to give them back (which was a good thing as I had already worn the panties when we had had it off in the cinema car park.)

I refused to read any more books that my mother brought back from the library for me, like *Lord of the Flies*, *Black Beauty*, *The Wonderful Wizard of Oz* and *Robinson Crusoe*, insisting instead on going alone to stock up on Mills and Boons. And I went up to the loft and brought down my old fairy-tale story books, like *Sleeping Beauty* and *Cinderella*.

When you stopped calling, I thought you had died. But when I saw you around, the shock was insurmountable. There must be something wrong with me. A prince doesn't leave a pretty girl to cry herself to sleep. That was for the cruel stepmother. The boy has to save the girl from misery and then they both live happily ever after. You couldn't have been a prince after all.

So I threw out my *Jackie*s and became a punk. I wore black eyeshadow and black lipstick, listening to Siouxsie and the Banshees and Joy Division. My heart now belonged to the Ice Queen.

But then I met Steve. He was tall, handsome and rebellious, *and* he had a motorbike. He liked Queen and smoked Rothmans. So we puffed away to 'Bohemian Rhapsody' and he melted my frozen heart with his lighter.

Mother's little legacy

I grew up not knowing my mother.

It was odd having her going insane in the attic, but I tried to forget she was there. Occasionally, she'd come down to take something from the fridge or walk up to my father and wail at him. Sometimes, I would go up there, to the attic, and find her in bed, knitting, or lying like a mummy, wrapped in a thermal blanket. If I tried to say something, she would wail at me, and hold out her hand to gesture me out.

I'd hear her once a month on a Sunday, taking a bath. Then she'd come down the stairs, dressed up and smelling of perfume. She wore a tight, red pencil skirt, tight, black jumper, black stockings and high heels. She'd take a cardboard box out onto the street, filled with jumpers and scarves she'd knitted for the local communist party fundraiser.

I would watch her through our front window, posing on the pavement, as though the whole world was watching her in awe. Eventually, a man drove up in a car and would take her box of knitwear. They'd talk before he drove away and she always stood there waving, until his car was out of sight. Then she'd come back in and go up again.

They say all women turn into their mothers, but, surely, I couldn't become someone I'd hardly known?

Then, one day, when I was forty, my father rang me to tell me she had died. I had to go through her things, because he couldn't bear to.

As I went up to the attic, I could smell my perfume. A black satin negligée was slung over the back of her chair. It was my size.

I sat at her mirror and her outline caught me like a ghost. My hair was the colour of hers. I heard my own voice coming back at me, wailing.

I told my father, 'I can't stay. I need to go back to my place, it's too eerie here.' My flat was cold so I quickly slipped on my negligée before wrapping myself in my thermal blanket and getting into bed. I could still smell her there with me. For the first time in my life I felt no longer alone.

When I woke in the morning I was late for work. I slipped off my negligée and with horror clocked that it was black satin. As I opened my wardrobe, I felt the same dread you would feel lifting the lid of the coffin of someone you loved. I could barely believe what I was doing as I took out my red pencil skirt and tight, black jumper, pulled up my black stockings, slipped on my heels and headed for the door.

Missing

All her life Julie felt like a vital part of her was missing. But like a missing child, the part, the missing part, was very much there. It demanded her attention, like an unsolved mystery. More flagrant than the other parts that were obviously there.

Optimistic as a school child, Julie had soon learnt that none of her teachers were even going to notice, let alone help her find, her vital part. On to university, through the reading of philosophy and psychology, she had searched for a clue; something a great sophist might have once said, that touched on the very nature of this lost piece. But on graduation she was no nearer to an answer.

By the age of 30 she had felt quite desperate. She needed to know if other people also felt they had misplaced something of themselves. So she asked them, young and old, educated and simple. And what she discovered was her salvation. Every single one of them knew what she was talking about. There wasn't, in fact, even one human being who didn't react with a, 'Yes! I have always felt that a vital part of me is missing.'

From then on, Julie accepted that feeling a part of you was missing was normal. She learned to live quite happily alongside this part, which she named Gertrude. She shared stories with her about her day and they had tea, and nights out at the cinema.

By the time she grew older, Julie's relationship with Gertrude had become quite one of co-dependence, with Julie being unable to fall asleep, or relax in front of the TV, without Gertrude there.

But, then, one day, Gertrude announced she was leaving. 'I feel like a vital part of me is missing,' she said.

The view

A young woman was lying on a beach when she was abruptly disturbed by an old barefooted woman in a bright cotton shawl.

'Are you enjoying yourself?', asked the old woman, peering down at her.

Startled, the young woman sat up and found herself looking into two deep, kind and mesmerizingly beautiful eyes.

'Yes, thank you,' she replied. 'I'm just soaking up the sun.'

Nodding, the old lady agreed. 'The sun is very good for you, isn't it?' she said.

'Yes, I only like the way I look when I have a tan. I don't like my natural, pale skin.'

'So, what have you given the sun in return for all your beauty?' asked the elder woman. But the young lady didn't understand what she meant and so the old woman went on her way.

Soon, she came across a couple of lovers, sitting on a sandy beach, enjoying the cool breeze from the sea. She stopped and greeted them both and then asked if they were enjoying themselves.

'Yes,' they said, their eyes sparking with passion. 'It's such a relief to come here, where the wind cools us down. It's too hot in the town!'

'So, what have you given the breeze, in return for the relief it has given to you?' asked the old lady. But the couple looked at her as though she were crazy and so she went on her way.

Lastly, she came upon an old man, kneeling by the side of a lake, staring down into the water. 'Hello,' she said. 'Are you enjoying yourself?'

'Not exactly enjoying,' he said. 'I have come here to find some calm in a crazy world. The water here is so still. It reflects back at me the stupidity of my never-ending worry.'

'So, have you given anything back to the lake over your many years, in return for this stillness of mind?' asked the old woman. But the man's eyes looked empty and he didn't say a word, so she went on her way.

A few years later disaster struck the earth. Forests and fields burned to the ground through lack of protection by man. The seas became polluted by human rubbish and most species were destroyed. The lakes dried up from soaring heat and there was little for anyone to drink. Only a few lucky ones survived to tell the tale, and I am one.

We've rebuilt our lives now but, this time, with respect for mother nature. We don't see her as there to provide for us, while never thanking her for all she gives. And when I come upon a beautiful view, I do not stare. I turn away as a mark of respect. By showing my back, the view knows it is only as vulnerable as I. It knows what we humans are like, and as quickly as I can draw my scythe, it can blow me over with a sudden gust of wind, or crack beneath my feet and let me fall to my death.

And, though the fields of green still roll, they do so without the weight of my eyes pinning them down. The grey-blue English waves still foam on the beach, but they're not doing so to calm me down. I know the view is still there behind me, but I let it cast its shadows on my back. And give it the space to dance naked, while I'm not looking.

Bla bla bla

We walk for a while, in silence. Then we turn a corner and a mountain with a man-made path to the peak lies ahead. Your muscles prime and you say, 'Ah! There is a fine mountain. It'll be fantastic to climb.'

And I think, 'Oh, there's a dreadful mountain. It'll be agony to climb.' My own muscles slump, and as we begin our ascent, while your legs hasten, as you look up to the top.

'The mountain is easy,' you enthuse, as your light steps pick up speed.

'I think it's hard,' I follow, while mine slow with the gathering of moss.

'A mountain is a natural land formation that rises in the form of a peak as an ever-increasing mass,' you tell me.

I am about to reply when comes the voice of a Tibetan, from 5,000 feet, above sea-level.

'Says who?' he calls down. 'A mountain doesn't rise. It descends, in the form of an ever-decreasing mass.' (ཨིན་ཏན་ཏན་རེ་མེག་མངས་སྤྱིར་སྤྱིར་ལྱ་ལྱག་རིང་ཨོ།)

You are about to reply when come the squawks of a mountain goose, from above the clouds, 23,000 feet above sea-level.

'Says who?' she laughs. 'You call that a mountain, but it's just a little spike!' ('Ahk ahk ahk ahk ahk. Kha kha kha kha kha.')

Continuing on our way, we shout our opinions upwards, to the Tibetan and the goose. But all they can hear is 'Bla bla bla bla bla.'

Rent-a-Hubby

As a woman living on her own, Kay had a love-hate relationship with DIY. Basically, she hated it. But if, as was very occasional, she did succeed at something, she grinned for weeks and told everyone about it. Shelves, though, were way out of her league. Spirit level, drill, sawing the wood to exactly the right width, buying the right wood in the first place…No.

So that's why she'd called Rent-a-Hubby. 'What a great name for a handyman,' she'd thought. 'Buzzing around in his white van, solving single women's DIY problems.' And he was due at any minute.

Kay checked herself in the mirror for the fourth time. A negligée was too clichéd and heavy makeup too obvious. A figure-hugging dress was OTT so she'd gone for the 'no make-up make-up', just got out of the bath look.

The white van screeched to a halt outside and she watched through her linen voiles as the epitome of masculinity whisked a heavy tool kit out of his boot with one hand and then slammed it shut with the flick of a little finger. As he strode up to her door, she could smell testosterone.

Pushing up her mascaraed eyelashes, she opened the door.

'Need some shelves putting up?' came a deep, husky voice, as Michelangelo's David cocked his head to one side.

'Come in,' Kay smiled, seductively raising her eyebrows and relishing the scent of his aftershave.

She let him walk first into the house so she could have a good look at his butt. Two bricks in worn Levi's, just like in her dreams. She pointed to the area that needed shelves and he immediately got to work.

'Cup a tea?' she chuckled. 'Or maybe something stronger?'

'S'alright thanks babe,' he said, eyes fixed only on the measurements he was marking on the wall. 'I got a thermos in the van.'

'Wife make you that, did she?'

He stopped, stood up and faced her. She melted at the sight of his lean hips. He folded his arms and cocked his head again. Coyly she bit her bottom lip.

'Don't have a wife,' he said dryly.

'Girlfriend?' she pouted, folding her arms to mirror his, then moving her thumbs inwards to stroke her own breasts.

He looked her up and down. 'What've you got under that towel, then?'

'I'll show you,' she grinned, and led him to the bedroom.

After they were finished, she realised she'd almost missed the supermarket.

'Got to nip out to the shops,' she said. 'Do you need anything?'

'You cooking tonight then?' he semi-joked. 'Some Stella would be sick. Cheers.'

'See you later,' she smiled and left him in her bed.

When she got back, he was watching football on TV, his feet up and one hand down his boxer shorts.

'You get the Stella?' he called after her, as she lugged the bags into the kitchen. She pulled out a can and took it to him.

'Thanks, hun,' he nodded, not taking his eyes off the ball.

'Who's playing,' she asked, but he didn't hear her.

'How are the shelves going?' she said.

'Oh, I'll do them tomorrow,' he muttered, mouth full of lager.

Martha the Great

Winston, the tall and charismatic chairman of the British Canine Institute, cleared his throat into the microphone.

Relied on for his generally excellent delivery of speeches, this elegant old bloodhound sat regally, his sail-like ears hanging heavily at the sides of his head. His worried and wise-looking forehead rolled over his eyes like two cinnamon swirls, and his huge mouth-flaps hung below his nose like heavy theatre curtains.

'Welcome everybody,' he began. 'I was delighted to be invited here today, as we gather to celebrate International Dog Day - the most important day of the year, of course!'

Hearty barking spread through the elegantly furnished hotel conference room, then waned in anticipation.

'I thought that I would take this opportunity,' he continued, 'to tell you about a brave and clever young woman; one of the most inspiring figures in modern history. A woman to whom we owe our very identities, as respected and much-loved companions within human society. Most, if not all, of you already know about Martha the Great, born at the University of Newcastle in 2036. But I would like to tell her story, nevertheless.'

'Hear, hear!' howled the crowd, as they lay to hear this very famous, treasured tale.

'For almost two centuries before Martha the Great, dogs held inside research laboratories, such as the one into which Martha was born, were prisoners of torture, fear and horror,' Winston began. 'Their chests were cut open so "scientists" could practice moving hearts from dog to dog or dog to human, as practice for surgery. Dogs' eyes were scalded with perfumes and make-up and cleaning materials. They were poisoned to make human medicines. They were kept in terrible conditions. Conditions not even fit for a cat. And, worst of all, the women had to watch as their babies were torn from their breasts and taken away, again and again and again.

'Martha the Great, herself, had forty babies taken. She told of how she could hear them whining for her on the other side of the wall. But, because she knew they would never be allowed to see her again, she didn't bark back. The quicker they forgot her the better.

'But by learning the humans' language, and then listening to and watching what they were doing, Martha the Great invented the way to save our species from a cruel life of slavery.

'It is said that the dogs she recruited, in the Newcastle laboratory, were so committed to her cause, that they practiced what she taught them, day and night. They knew their own lives couldn't be saved, but they did what they did in the name of future generations. And here we all are!

'You will have heard of the famous epigenetics experiment. The dogs had been divided into two groups. One group was given electric shocks while the smell of cherry blossom was pumped into their crates. The second group only received the cherry blossom smell. No shocks. They were the lucky ones.

'The scientists discovered that the babies of the electric shock group, even though they had never seen their parents, and had been raised in a different building, were born frightened of the smell of cherry blossom. It had been proved that traumatic memory can be passed on in the genes.

'The human researchers became so overwhelmed with excitement, at their incredible breakthrough study, that they talked non-stop about their findings. They repeated and finely-tuned their experiments, until they were talking all day about winning the next Nobel-prize. What they didn't realise was that Martha had taught the dogs English. And they were listening.

'Martha the Great's ancestors, like many laboratory dogs, had been bred for obedience. They had always done what they were told and never questioned or complained. However badly they were treated by their people, they stayed loyal to the end. They had no genes for anger, nor rebellion.

'But Martha had seen, from the experiment in which she herself had been part, that dogs inherited behaviours from their forebearers. Now what she needed to do was create situations which would galvanise the behaviour they needed to cultivate.

'So, day after day, night after night, when no one was watching, she taught the dogs to feel angry about their dreadful circumstances. She encouraged them to get mad with rage, insulting them and mimicking them and also making sure they knew all about the terrible things that were happening inside the laboratory. Generation after generation, the dogs became angrier and angrier as the anger was passed to their offspring. And then, one day, the dogs became so furious when people approached their crates, they could be handled by humans no longer.

'After a few months of trying, and failing, to tame the, now, vicious animals, the scientists had to abandon the whole idea of using dogs ever again. All dogs in laboratories were freed, and laws were passed preventing the use of dogs, due to their unsuitable nature when captive.

'Martha the Great's wisdom and wit, as well as the sacrifice of the dear, selfless dogs who helped her, won us all our freedom. Now we live out our lives in warm and loving human homes, in comfy baskets and fed for free. Thanks to her, no dog will ever again be tortured in the name of science, for medicines, or transplants or human make-up.

'I raise my glass to Martha. Hip Hip, Hooray, for Martha the Great!'

My opinion

I am intricately constructing a work in progress and will defend it to the death.

Without it I would be as lost as if I were to venture from my hometown. It is my opinion.

You say, 'It's this way!' with your guidebook, shaking it in my face. Rectangular blocks of print. Black and white stripes. Drawing me in, in Zs, as my eyes follow from left to right.

You try to talk your way in, and try to talk your way out. But I don't believe any of it. It's just fiction.

You sing your solo song, all lies and lullabies. You'd like to soothe me to sleep, to dream your dream. But I like mine.

Ask me to prove myself, though, and I will slink away. I will not even try to demonstrate my God is really there. Not even with all the words in the world. Because I can't prove it is. Just as you can't prove it isn't.

The arboreal revolution

The children had just had a history lesson, about a time before people lived in the trees. A time when humans lived on the plains and controlled everything. Even the other animals.

Slim, a tall and elegant African boy, had found it hard to believe that humans could survive out there on the dry savannahs, as his teacher had said was so. But he trusted the professor, who had seen a book from that very time.

As he lazed in the crook of his favourite mahogany, Slim tried to picture how it must have been; how scorched by the sun they must have felt, with no forest to provide cool and shade. And not being able to travel through the branches at breakneck speed must have been really boring.

He was a thinker, this graceful African boy, happiest at the top of the tallest tree, watching over the forest as if he were a great eagle. And as he lay imagining the past, the crowns of the highest mahoganies scooped up the rays of the early evening sun and stopped them falling to the ground.

The history teacher had told them that the era when people lived on the ground had ended when they'd overheated the planet with gas, and then dropped bombs that set half the world on fire. Only a few had survived, and they were his distant relatives.

During their lesson, the teacher had told them a story about a wise old grandfather from that time. The grandfather had saved his family from the fires and wars. He was sitting with his children and his grandchildren around him, telling them to prepare themselves for a long journey. This grandfather, even though his eyes were clouded by cataracts and his ears were full of hair, understood much about survival.

'As you know, we humans can walk for many days at a time,' he had told the children. 'In fact, you are very well designed for that. But, here on the plains we are vulnerable, and visible to predators of all kinds. And we crave more shade from the harsh sun. So, we are going to walk for a very long time. We will walk until we come upon a rainforest. And there we will settle forever.'

But the children had so many questions, just as Slim himself would have had if he'd been one of them.

'Why a rainforest?' one daughter had asked.

'Because we're going back to the trees.'

'To live in! Like monkeys and birds?!' said a grandson.

'Yes,' said the grandfather. 'Because there we will always have the advantage of being 'uphill'. We'll be shielded from the sun yet will never go short of rain. We'll build tree houses, and hang fires from the branches, to keep us warm and cook our food. We'll feast on fruits and game and guard the forest edge day and night.'

'Grandfather, how do you mean go *back* to the trees?' the old man's daughter had asked. 'Have we not always lived on the land?'

'Not at all!' said the grandfather. 'Have you not been listening in history? We come from the trees. We evolved from the apes who once lived in them, and who we may well find still do. And, if they do, they'll become our friends in times to come, you'll see.'

'But,' the old man's son asked, 'how could we have once been monkeys when all monkeys can do is swing from the branches? How come we had legs with feet to walk back onto the plains?'

'Now, don't you go mixing up apes with monkeys!' said the grandfather. 'Monkeys have tails but apes do not. Do you have a tail? No. Because you're an ape, not a monkey. Apes can walk very well on their feet. You will find out for yourself before long. We can swing from branches, too. It's just something you've never learned.'

As he lay recalling the story, Slim was distracted by a faint smell of cooking, that wafted from his village across the forest canopy. 'Dinner time!' he smiled. He was about to hurl himself from one tree to the next, but he paused. Then, rather than jump, he carefully slid himself all the way down the trunk to the ground. 'Like a snake,' he thought.

'It's really hard to imagine not flying through the branches when you want to get somewhere,' he mulled, putting one foot in front of the other on the forest floor. 'But, actually,' he found, 'I quite like walking upright.'

As his bare feet found their way home, between the trunks, Slim could sense there were many more layers of geology beneath him than he had previously known to be there. In fact, he realised, he was walking upon his ancestors.

Ring of fire

We both know, my love, that there is a ring of fire through which we could jump. And that, on the other side, lies freedom.

I sense your fear that I will leave you here. That one day you will find I am gone. That I jumped through, deep at night, as you lay sleeping in our ordinary bed. And that I have found a better world without you.

And I know you think you cannot jump. Because, like me, you are plagued by a memory huger than that of all the other poor creatures that snivel on this three-dimensional earth.

Last night I watched you as you stoked the fire. As the flames started to gather their own momentum, just that tiny bit taller and wilder than you had thought, how quickly a single human memory was, to leap, uninvited, into your moment. To defend you, like a reincarnated knight from your dismembered past. Sliding his primeval sword from its sheath, whispering 'Danger', slyly, under your breath.

And, not, as one might think, because you were ever burned. So, not for a recollection of that searing prick, then the seething heat, first jubilantly crackling across the hairs of the skin, then boring down, gravely, to the soft white flesh below. But, rather, because, one fine day, your mother or your father, tugged you harshly away from their fire, scolding you with wagging fingers, not to go near it because 'Fire Can Kill You'.

But don't fear, my love, that I will leave you for the fears that you feel, and the U-turns you take. I, too, am a simmering mass of memories, that goad me in circles with no end. I, too, hide a fearful interferer, who tells me I am going the wrong way. I, too, blindly follow a path set out before me, stepping cautiously along the words I heard as I first grew. Here on the safe side of the ring of fire.

Plenty of fish

As she walked away after thirty years of marriage, she said, 'Next time, choose someone simple.'

She had emigrated to America one day, to be with another woman.

After she had left him, he sat on a shelf in the seafront flat they had shared, and thought, 'Yes, she was very complicated. Maybe I need someone simpler.'

He stayed there for a year, his skin thickening and drying, like a drumskin in the desert, his muscles shortening and stiffening at the thought of what his wife was doing. Her little messages came from across the Atlantic. How was he? She wanted the best for him. She would always love him, but not like *that*. Those words weren't new. She hadn't desired him for a decade, and his body still felt crushed, like a written off car. Nothing pumped and nothing filled or drained.

But, after twelve long months, he decided he was ready to dip his toe in the waters of online dating. He turned to 'Plenty of Fish', an online sea of hearts, where hundreds of them thumped along brightly in a sea of blushing hope.

'Choose someone simple,' came her voice from the depths.

But he shrugged the voice off and dived in to find the shoals. Pretty and ugly bait awaited. He sniffed at their scales for something special to lock on to, but they were all too silky and smooth, and slipped over his bumpy, barnacled surface.

But then, just as he was about to retreat to land and hang his battered bathing gear to dry, he saw her. A regal little fish, with multi-coloured protrusions and a changing face. His huge eyes didn't blink as he swam straight towards her. 'What is happening?' he thought, as her finger-like projections delved through the holes in his armour and locked him fast upon her.

'Have I found my antidote?' he flirted with her coyly.

'But she's not simple!' bellowed the voice from below. 'Look at all those fancy projections and that ever-changing face!'

'Hmmm,' he thought. 'Yes, she does look a bit complicated. Maybe I do need someone simpler.' So, he turned and skulked away, swimming sideways and backwards and in circles; in any way that got him away from her.

But then what happened was a surprise. As he neared the land, he found that he was loose and moist in a way he had forgotten. His muscles were long and lithe and his chest felt wide and open. The dark holes in his pitted surface yearned for more rainbow-coloured light to fill them. This time he felt as if he was swimming with the ocean, not against it.

So, he turned sharply around and thrashed out into the depths again, this time knowing what he was looking for. Multi-coloured projections and a changing face. But, although she was still there, floating alone in a sea of dashed dreams, she knew he could never find her. Because her face was only sad now and she was just the colour of the sea.

Good old Alfred

Alfred nestled back, cross-legged, into his haggard armchair. A threadbare, leg-shaped, patch had been worn into the seat cushion under his left thigh, where it had nestled every hour since his wife, Mavis, had died.

Beside him stood a desk, invisible for the perilously high piles of journals, pamphlets and books, some of which had collapsed into wads that looked like archeological expedition sites.

'Bloody animal,' he scorned, as a thin and mangy tortoiseshell banged clumsily through its flap, and plodded sheepishly through the kitchen, each step bearing a muddy print left visible on the stone floor.

'Never done a bloody day's work in your life, you scrounging piece of contagious vermin.' The cat crouched low and sunk its spine, then skulked warily out of sight.

Mavis's brain tumour had left Alfred to live out his long, remaining days in the village bungalow they had bought when their city life had proved too dazzling for her and she had requested no more than a view over fields.

Alfred and Mavis' s city apartment had once bubbled with the fresh, boiling blood of idealistic young politicos, angry trade unionists, anarchic students and far-left socialists. Once a distinguished economics lecturer, Alfred's lifelong passion had been to educate students, voters, neighbours, friends and the young alike, about the need for a revolution by the working classes to overthrow the calamitous trap that was capitalism. His three celebrated works, on communism, anarchism and

Leninism, were placed in prime position in the centre of his battered desk. But, they, too, were now concealed by browning papers and thoroughly devoured manifestos.

In a village of no particular significance, ten miles from the city, Alfred felt surrounded by apathy, individualism and mindless commercialism. He was aghast at the apolitical ignorance of the villagers. No one stopped by to ask how he was. No one was interested in hearing about the perforation of the Iron Curtain, nor the hacking and hammering of the Berlin Wall by gullible imbeciles. No one was apparently conscious of the fact that they were spellbound by capitalist advertising, nonsensical promises and vicious lies. Families born in the village rarely visited the city for cultural reasons, let alone left the country or even county. They simply grew and shrunk, following the repetitious path from birth to death.

Now that Alfred's optimism, that the government could be overthrown, had waned chronically with his years, he faced an intolerable lack of purpose, and, with it, the deepening understanding that his existence had been utterly futile. No longer a host for gatherings of comrades, he despaired at the recreational values of others, the absurd unproductiveness of retirement and the nauseating frivolity of weekends.

Still cross-legged in his armchair, Alfred conjured up a picture of Mavis's smiling face. 'Ah, Mavis' he muttered, as he reached over an open hardback to grasp for the whiskey bottle. 'I'm ready for the worms.'

**stories
grey**

.

Catharsis

It was just going to be a story about how guilty I felt. Guilty for ending the relationship. And hurting you. Leaving you.

I recall the days when I started the book; they were petrol blue. The colour, I think, of guilt. From the first light of dawn to the last light of dusk, as I wrote and wrote, that noxious blue imbibed the hours, as if all bright things, like the sun and the moon and the stars, had been engulfed by petrol-scented air.

But as I wrote those early chapters, in the blue smog, I began to see how the relationship breakdown had not all been my fault. That it wasn't only me to blame. That the things I'd said and done, as things were going wrong, weren't cold, or indifferent, but actually understandable. And as I wrote each word, it was as if a grain of sand was lifted off the sorry scale and placed, instead, on to an angry scale.

I recall the days when I wrote the angry chapters; they were red. Fiery red, while the anger raged and blood red as I took my revenge. My pen became so hot it burned my fingers. Incidents where it was you, not me, that had been the cruel one, took form. I described the shocking steel in your eyes as you'd lift your hand to slap me, and how I'd cry for hours after.

But because it was only a story, I could defend myself. So, instead of cowering like a victim, I imagined thumping you, as hard as I could, into your solar plexus. Then kicking you wildly down the cellar stairs so you tumbled and spun onto the hard stone floor beneath. I imagined you lying at the bottom, your neck cocked hard against your shoulder. Dying, perhaps.

But, one day I woke to find that the, by then, familiar blood-red sunrise was the orange of embers. I panicked, and ran to find the man still lying at the bottom of the stairs. I looked into his glazed and melancholy eyes and saw only the vulnerable little boy you once told me all about; still making amends for the beatings you received at the hands of a drunken father.

So, I crouched beside you and dragged you by the shoulders onto my lap. I didn't want you to die. I held your head and cried for a while, then pulled you up the stairs and into our bed. And then the story became about you. I nursed the pain and bruises until you were well. They were purple days and purple words – the colour, I think, of pity.

By the time you were strong again and ready to go your own way, it felt as if I were nearing the end of the book. It had been a better tale for seeing it from more than just one point of view. And, if the ending was a mystery to the writer, just like life, then all the better.

So, I picked up the phone and called you, not knowing what you'd say. "Hi. Good to hear from you," you said. "What've you been up to?"

"Just writing," I said. But as I heard that voice of yours I so adored, the purple pity lightened to a glorious pink. The colour, I think, of love.

"How are you feeling?" you asked.

I could have said, "Guilty. Angry. Pitying." But that was written now. It was time for the last line.

"I... I just... love you," I said.

Wonderful world

The last time I saw Mum, three paramedics were wheeling her into an ambulance, muffled by their masks in the silent street.

Between her laboured breaths she chuckled,
'Tata, then'
as the doors slammed shut. And as they sirened away, I realised
I'd forgotten to say
goodbye.

Early that evening I got a phone call from the hospital. Mum had been moved to ICU and put on a ventilator.

The next morning, a different person rang. They were so, so, sorry, but Mum's condition had worsened overnight
and there was
no more they could do.

'Is she alive?' I bawled. She was, but wasn't going to make it.

Heartbeat in my head, I grasped to put my shoes on without dropping the phone.
'What's the name of the ward? Oh my God! Where do I go? Where do I park?'

But the stranger on the phone told me that visitors weren't allowed.
'I'm not just a visitor, she's my mum!'
I cried. 'She can't be all alone! I need to be with her!'

'I will hold her hand,' said the stranger,
and we both wept.

I had always pictured my mum's death. A cheery hospice, bed by a window, overlooking fields. A summer's day. A blackbird singing. Daffodils and Lilies in a vase. I'd sit beside her, stroking her forearm, holding her hand. And in those dying moments, I'd find the guts to say the hardest words:

'I love you.'

I'd say 'I'm sorry,' too. For all the things I'd said and done and wished I hadn't. And she'd say, 'Oh, don't be daft! I'd forgotten anyway.'

And I'd be holding her hand
and stroking her forehead.
And I'd weep.

But then, she'd lift her arm and wipe the tears from my cheek and ask me to tell her a funny joke. 'How about the one with Jesus and John?' she'd ask, chuckling.

And she would wait. So, I'd say: 'And the Lord said, unto John, "Come forth, and you will receive eternal life!" But John came fifth and won a toaster.' And how we'd giggle until it hurt, but then her laughter would fade into a smile,
and she'd ask me to sing her favourite song…

♬   I see trees of green
Red roses too
I see them bloom
For me and you
And I think to myself
What a wonderful world   ♬

50

The phone rang. He said he was a doctor. 'I'm so very sorry
to have to tell you this, but,
your mother, she
passed
away,
a few minutes ago.'

'I know!' I said. 'I was right there, wasn't I. Singing to her. Holding
her hand.'

Free

It is a quarter to four. I hang at four.

I have known, for what felt like eternity, that I am to be hanged for a crime I didn't commit. And I was OK until they put a clock in my cell.

I had reached a state of transcendence, where I could close my eyes and see anything I wanted. I prayed, and I visualised the place I might go after here, or the place I came from before.

But this clock they've hung, it chains me down to earth. It ticks in my mind and, however hard I try not to let it, it stops any vision lasting more than a second. One second. A unit, now, of death, not of life. I am forced to hear the seconds disappear. I have been pitted against time.

I have tried to move in rhythm with the hand that ticks, and dance a perpetual, incarnate dance. I've tried to see my life so far, as a motorway. And I am just a car. And, yes, once in a while someone crashes. And this would be no worse than that, if it weren't for the knowing when. Now, it's like I'm on the motorway, passing signs that say, 'You will crash and die in seven days, 10 hours and 50 minutes.' 'You will crash and die in one day, one hour and 10 minutes. You will die in 45 seconds. Etc.'

It is four o'clock.

Now it's a minute past four, and they haven't come. Could it be that the clock was wrong?

Then the familiar clank of the latch and male voices drown out the ticking of the second hand. I fall to my knees, not in despair, but in praise. The walls of my cell start to widen. The low ceiling rises to form a vault, and the small slit in my wall becomes a magnificent stained-glass window. My door opens, and instead of wardens, there are huge angels standing there. Beckoning me to follow them.

I am free.

The year without a summer

That year, the green and golden fields miscarried, leaving only trickles of mud in the soil.

No flowers rose above the earth and the bees kept what honey they had for themselves.

Wine was rationed and driven underground, while cafés and bars closed their shutters. The people fought and the weakest fell or were crushed under the feet of the fit.

Trees and bushes froze immobile, as statues, like photographs, suspended out of time, unable to unfold in the sun.

The animals died in silence, dropping humbly one by one, flat onto the fields, visible only, from afar, as a carpet of bony brown across the land.

Now, love is possible in both summer and winter, but only Eros in summer and Philautia in winter. And so it was that every lover died, as judgement and separation fueled the battle for survival.

Next to succumb was the community. Conversations on street corners ceased as doors were locked against the cold, and errands were run in the rain.

For when the head is bowed, the heart is hidden and when corners of mouths fall southward, heavy and loaded and leaded, the mind wants to weep and the soul wants to sleep, and it is as if the heart wants to stop beating forever.

So through that dark year, in the moments of meeting, the eyes of good people did not bear to bare themselves, so as not to give too much away. The heaviness and grief at the loss of summer were too deep, too raw, so not, then, to be shared. Each solitary spirit withered on its way through the clouds, unwilling, as we are in England, to bleed in the dark of day.

Human eyes in summer, they gleam and they sparkle and dance with reflections of warmth and the light. Their colours show true, the colours beneath the colours, within the colours, as they bare more and more of the soul.

And in the summer our bodies they dance a dance of love. As spontaneity reveals creation. In the moment, in the sun.

But eyes in the dark are hidden and unseen. They withdraw with the blues. Wasted, lonely, yet pleading for a salvation they know will never come. Their true colours are lost without light, the colour doesn't matter anymore, as the ever further sinking of the soul sees nothing ahead but the end.

And so it was in the year without a summer, the year we call zero, when everything died leaving nothing but autumn, and winter… and spring!

The court

All of a sudden, a huge gust of wind lifted her cotton dress to her waist. She tried to pin it down, so her bottom wouldn't show, but needed one hand to protect her face from the straps of her long dark hair that whipped on it like cat-o'-nine-tails.

Before she could even think what to do, a tremendous roar rose behind her and she was sucked into the vortex of a huge tornado. Tumbling in its belly across a thousand rooftops she saw a large and magnificent building below. And there, she was dropped, right down, through its roof, and into the middle of a wood-paneled room full of people acting extremely seriously.

The first thing she noticed was the way they were dressed. Heavy, stiff, angular costumes made them look bigger than they really were. She imagined how, even in the full force of a storm, those type of clothes would prevent people from being blown away.

The folk around her could be divided into three groups. Firstly, well-built, dressed in black, with round helmets, big boots and, at their sides, holsters, batons and grenades.

Second were a group of greying ladies, with wrinkled faces and unflattering clothes. She thought she caught a slight flicker of empathy from one of them but was swiftly overwhelmed by expressions that suggested she had done something she shouldn't have.

Lastly, was the group of posh-suited, rich-looking people, shuffling through huge stacks of papers and whispering to one another. They didn't much spare a moment to even look in her direction.

A door opened at the front of the room as a voice hailed, 'All rise.' Everyone froze silent, as a man wearing a sheep wig appeared through the door and walked sternly up some steps and onto a stage. The man sat down in what looked like a throne, and cleared his throat. Then, he peered right down at the girl, and said, in a voice with no intonation, 'Are you the defendant?'

Craning her neck as far as she could to try and meet his eye, the girl replied, 'What is a defendant?', hoping very much that it was an OK thing to say.

Truthsayer

In this life, some things people say are true and some are lies.

When you start out on life's marathon, it will be hard to tell the difference. You will start by believing everybody.

But you are not a truthsayer. Nor can you see the bitten tongues behind the soft and luring smiles. You're not a polygraph that counts in heartbeats and measures in breaths. You're just a human. And, at the end, you'll wonder, 'Was it all a lie? Did I lie to myself? Did I lie to everyone?'

As you approach the finishing line, truth will be there, holding out a foil blanket. She's like the wall still standing when the war is over, littered with bullet holes. She shielded you from the crossfire, and from yourself. And if you did catch a bullet, she healed the cuts you were too ashamed to face.

Lie, though, she blinded you, an eye, here. She broke you, a heart, there. She spewed your guts out everywhere. She dulled your light in case you burned yourself, and you believed her because she was a part of you.

Thankfully, lies must stay behind, at the end of this nasty, brutish, short human life. Where it is as easy to disbelieve the truth as it is to believe a lie. Only truth you take with you when you go.

From Adam

It was around 10pm. The open plan penthouse was haunted by swathes of blue light from the security cameras that pointed into the apartment. Jared, a fit young man in his mid-thirties lay awake and agitated, in his empty king size bed. His dark, shoulder length, wavy hair was damp with sweat. Under a single sheet he was nude.

'Air con turbo,' he shouted, sitting up and wedging the pillows from the other side of the bed behind his back. A whirring sound got louder and faster and circulating air created a ripple effect on the hairs of his chest and head.

'I'm sick of this,' he moaned to the empty room. 'I can't remember when I last had a good night's sleep.'

'Five nights ago,' came a gentle but upbeat female voice from somewhere within the walls. 'You took a Zinox.'

'Oh yeah,' Jared sighed. 'Nero, can I have one in the tray, please.'

'One moment…Yes,' said a perfunctory male voice from the dispensing machine across the room.

Jared pulled his legs round and placed his feet on the glossy stone floor. As he stepped, skin sensors activated two paths of pale white lights ahead of him like a mini runway. He stood, stark naked, and walked towards the dispenser. A small blue light flashed several times before a tiny blue packet fell down onto a black plastic tray. 'Your Zinox. Dosage as specified at previous request. For altered dosage, please ask Wilby.'

Jared pinched the package with his fingers and slid it between his cheek and his teeth. He closed his eyes and sighed. There was no expression on his face. Barely opening his eyes, he walked back to the bed, climbed in and wearily fell back onto the stack of pillows.

'How long 'til this thing works?' he asked.

'Twelve minutes,' replied the comforting woman's voice he was so familiar with.

'OK, well that just about gives us time to request a date for tomorrow evening, Wilby.' He looked pained, rubbing his forehead and screwing up his eyes. 'The usual please. Show me the best you got.'

'That's single, 26-35, not looking for relationship, no kids, any hair colour, professional, right?'

'Yeah.'

'Time?'

'Six.'

'Zone?'

'A or B.'

A large flatscreen TV flashed the image of a smartly dressed, tanned brunette, pouting pensively at a work desk, wearing a dark fitted jacket and white feminine blouse, her slender fingers weighted down with huge gold rings.

'She looks hot!' Jared exclaimed, sitting more upright now and starting to rejuvenate. 'Nice work Wilby. Rating?'

'Four'

'Oh. Why so low?'

'Reviews aren't great. You want the latest?'

'Sure.'

'Hard work, never relaxes, no conversation.'

'Pfffffff. Previous.'

'Too much makeup, uptight.'

'Previous.'

'Frigid. No extras.'

'Ooooof. But she looks hot. Bed rating, Wilby.'

'Six.'

'Accessibility.'

'All positions. No extras.'

'5D.'

The image of the lady converted to a hologram which started to spin slowly.

'Great arse. Financial?'

'Undisclosed. But on the basis of reviews, not good. Refused to pay for dinner or drinks on several occasions.'

'Can you scan the body for fat, please Wilby.'

'33%'

'Urh. Bit high. Where is it?'

'Stomach, back and upper arms largely.'

'Dimensions?'

'98, 83, 100, knee 29, calf 27.'

'She matched me?'

'I only show you matches, remember.'

'Yeah. Um. What's the return rate?'

'90%'

'Ffffff. Over what period?'

'Six years, with two years, two months offline.'

'Ah. Who with?'

'Uhhhhh, no, he's Platinum, so we don't have access.'

'Photo of mother.'

An image of a prim, portly woman in her 60s popped up beside the one of her daughter.

'Father.'

A round pallid man in his 60s, with a smooth face lacking features, sitting behind a desk with a flag.

'Mother's a dog, father's a trout. But she is HOT, Wilby. Look at those breasts!'

'They're implants.'

'Who cares. Vagina?'

'Internal, average. External tidy, mostly Californian.'

Jared stared motionless at the hologram.

'I like this girl.'

'Why?'

'I have no idea.' He pauses. 'Request her.'

Wilby interrupted. 'Hold on Jared you're rushing in here. Let's check her background at least.'

'Oh Wilby,' Jared sighed, 'you sound like my mother.'

'Hang on a minute Gold has expired. We need to upgrade.'

'You mean, I need to, Wilby. I'm paying. How much?'

'Gold is £55 a week or £150 for the month. And, in my opinion, worth it. Could be a pirate profile.'

'OK.'

'Upgraded to Gold. Running checks for med history. Criminal records, social media. OK. Criminal record - 2065 shoplifting, 2067 fraud....'

'What was the fraud?'

'Stolen credit card. Wo, check this out. Prostitution.'

'When?'

'2070. £20,000 fine and two years unpaid military service.'

'Wo. So, there's skeletons.'

'Med history - ongoing - Piles. Lymphoma in left breast, 2095, left breast, single mastectomy, cryotherapy, resolved. History - Gonorrhea, hepatitis C, clinical depression, prescribed Prozac, manic depressive disorder managed with lithium, hysterical personality diagnosed 2071, attempted suicide twice in 10 years...'

'Christ, that's enough Wilby. Do your research next time, OK?'

'Sorry, sir, but I needed your authorisation for the upgrade.'

'Yeah, Wilby, Yeah. I'll just go out. Down to a hotel bar. Look for something with a pulse.'

'That's so last century, Jared. You won't know them from Adam.'

'Who knows. Maybe I'll be nicely surprised.'

**stories
black**

Everyone

Everyone, at some time or another, sits down to a banquet of consequences.

'To start with, your hors d'oeuvre, madame,' announced the waiter, as he lifted the heavy silver lid. 'A son - sharp-witted, sensitive, tall and lean. Twelve weeks in your womb before you poisoned him and had him siphoned out to be discarded as clinical waste.'

'Thank you,' I said.

'And for your soup,' he continued, 'Your mother.' 'Pardon? Pardon?' she bleats, as she strains to hear what is being said around her, so wanting to, so needing to, but unable to. Because, in my teenage rage, I lashed my cupped palm against the side of her head, bursting the air through her ear drum and leaving her deaf in that ear forever more.

'Much obliged,' I said.

'And next, for your main,' continued monsieur le serveur, 'Your father, his lower eyelids drooped so deep you can see inside to the balls. His back so bowed and crooked from carrying you that he bent so far forwards one day, he tumbled into his own grave.'

'You're very kind,' I said.

'And for dessert,' he went on, 'may I present a selection of your wedding dresses, worn only once, left to feed the moths and with no husband still to show for any of them.'

'Very nice,' I said.

'And lastly, madame, a selection of mignardises, on the 'ouse. Some enemies with grudges in the absence of your apologies; lovers forever scarred by your callousness; homes sold and neighbours left behind; and gardens, gardens of weeds.'

'Oh, you really shouldn't have,' I said.

'And, finally, if madame is ready for her dessert wine?'

'No! I am not!' I said.

I ran out into the night and fell onto my hands and knees on the cold damp lawn. I wretched. Until everyone, everything, I had ever loved, lay partly digested below me. Then I tore every blade and stalk from the ground and sucked at the stalks and chewed on the leaves. Until the sap dripped down my throat, into my cells, like green light.

Letter

She grits her teeth and rolls onto her side, to grasp for the plastic pen on her bedside table. Unable to find it with her fingers, she forces open one eyelid at a time, against the weight of the shame. But chinks of light scrabble through the bedroom curtains and scorch the comfort of her darkness. The lids fall again, and she follows. Back into the noxious hollow of her bed.

The sound of children in a school playground can be heard faintly outside. 'Life goes on, for some,' she thinks, screwing up her eyes to quash the pictures that taunt her when they can. Pictures of them. Together. Him, aroused, kneeling over her. Kissing her cheeks and nose. His hands all over her golden locks.

'All those years as a family' she struggles. 'What a way for our marriage to end.'

Primed for a fight, her muscles splint her in a vice. She only breathes to avoid asphyxiation. The images flow like setting concrete along her neural networks then down her throat, through her guts and into her shaky hand. 'I thought we had good sex. You seemed to enjoy it, to me,' she self-comforts.

She reaches out for the pen again, her fingers like the feeble pincers on a steel toy crane in an amusement arcade. She brushes the hard plastic with her fingernail, then pinches it hard, and yanks it towards the writing paper on her lap. A last letter.

'Dear Lawrence.' No, strike "Dear". I cannot call you "Dear".' "Lawrence, I just want you back." 'No. Strike that. People will think I'm sick in the head.'

Her knickers on the pillow. Her dress on the floor.

"Lawrence, I'm struggling to understand how you could do this." 'No, strike that. What's the point?'

"Lawrence, it's time I left this house, this city. I'm taking Grace and we're moving away. Please don't come looking for us. You've damaged her enough. I managed to get her a school place at the local school where we're going. Think of her with her whole life ahead of her. Maybe she'll come find you one day when she's older. If she ever forgets how you molested her."

"p.s. I love you." 'No. Strike that.'

Bloody mess

It burst through her pelvic floor, rupturing the pink perineum into two chunks of fissured flesh, hanging helplessly between her legs.

Limp and languid, they lifted it from its pool of blood into the sour-smelling air. Pressure piled upon its chest and it stalled, suffocating, still as death, on the brink of life.

Blinding light bled into its eyes but, sensing danger, it squeezed them soundly shut. It cared only for its dark past.

Voices rose and fell around it, commanding it into this world, assuming life necessarily followed birth. Six blue plastic hands lunged at its belly with burnished blades, rupturing the rope, cutting the cord. It hollered a Munchian scream.

They thrust it onto its mother until its own smell calmed it down. The mother's every muscle twitched as she tried to jam her nipple through its bared gums. Her leeched chest bled from its bite. Her heart was empty. She could all but bother to breathe. 'This baby doesn't love me,' she thought.

She had no memories of ever having had a mother. All she'd known were her father's advances and demands. There, on the maternity ward, was the first time in her life she hadn't been held captive in a locked room, the first time she had slept in a comfortable bed.

She slept that night like a baby, unaware of the indigent creature wedged between the mattress and the tucked sheet beside her.

But in the cold light of day, all the two of them could do was cry.
Ball and sob, blubber and wail.
Between the bouts, all she could feel was her heartbeat thumping.
She cowered under the covers, sinking in her own sweat.
She camouflaged it with the covers.
She wandered around the ward and back, wanting to run but being drawn back.
She stood up and sat down, stood up and sat down.
She tried to get back into the bed but it was there, taking up all the space.
She held a pillow over its head until it was quiet.
And then she cried, again.
But, this time tears of joy.
At the whole new life that lay ahead of her.

Disengagement

Bella peered blankly into their bathroom mirror.

The only face she saw was hers.

'You shouldn't have left me at this age,' she sobbed.

'You shouldn't leave someone once they've lost their looks.'

Every part of her hurt, independently from the rest, but all joined up like a jigsaw puzzle of pain, threatening to fall apart, with pieces missing.

She wore her husband's deceit like armour. The armour of shame, the shame of abandonment.

She bore the silence like a pneumatic drill. The silence of being unlovable. It hadn't been clean, his deceit. You couldn't say that at least she hadn't suffered. He was a cluster bomb.

There'd been no drama. No bruises. He'd left no evidence for her to rely on. Nor memories. His betrayal was miserably slow and insidious. Corrosive in its injuries. The torture was that he just didn't care anymore. Didn't pay her any attention. Could imagine a future without her.

She held her belly with the pain. His was the worst kind of betrayal. Covert. Intangible. Invisible.

Disengagement.

Black dog

She was terrified of the future.

She would have much preferred to stay right there, forever. Where no one would see her feeble, sluggish figure as it rocked and flinched in wanton inertia.

But, even with her eyes closed, she couldn't prevent time from cavorting ahead, sucking her physical mass along its tunnel vortex of helicoid spirals, luminous within an infinite blackness.

Like a dilapidated morsel of meat, an itinerant within time's gut, she was trapped by its omnipotence. Her back was glued to its intestinal walls with the centrifugal force of peristalsis. And as she passively dissolved in hydrochloric acid, her nutrients sept languidly into the rivers of blood that nourished its vital organs.

She knew that, like the worms that crept under the earth, and the trees that sucked up water though their roots, she was just another morose automaton, estranged from the force that drove the world to spin, her hair to grow, and people to meet and fall in love.

Like the hostages living in the flat above, who compulsively banged and thumped and laughed and cried and clinked and clanked at the washing up, whose front door slamming sent shockwaves through her bones, as they devoutly hailed amongst themselves the importance of their comings and goings.

And, like the black dog, that plodded predictably along the pavement above her basement flat. A miserable pawn of a victim, whose only joys were the sniffing of urine and the opening of its bowels. But who, defenceless against the curse of an owner afflicted by an impetuous inability to stand still, was never granted enough time to complete either process. But, rather, was mercilessly dragged away, mid-flow or mid-movement, throttled by a choker that gouged into its Adam's apple.

She wondered what the joy of an empty bladder might have felt like to the wretched mongrel. Or the bliss of an evacuated rectum. Joy, she had realised, was not something you were born with, but something you had to acquire. And she, herself, had not been able to acquire it. It was like asking a mouthless baby to cry or a baker to make bread without flour.

What she did know, for sure, though, was that she would never feel joy. Because things never changed. They'd been like this for so long now, how could they?

Silent seconds

When I wake up, the other side of the bed is cold.

As I push my palm against the same smooth sheets the coolness there feels like a hole. But for some few beautiful seconds, I bask in the peace that follows sleep. The unknowing of all life's pain, in those first blissful moments after waking.

I reach down to feel for you, ready to play. My fingers uncurl like petals searching for signs of light in the darkness of our bed. But instead of the tingle of desire, a harsh, shrill playground bell clangs and bangs me back. A cursed call, a repellant reminder that you have left me. And that she may be holding you now. And again, my heart sinks, back, down, down. Into the crevasse between my breasts.

You used to bring me a cup of tea when we woke. All I had to mouth was 'tea', or I would simply draw the letter T on your back. And you would go and make me tea, while I dozed in dreams until I heard your feet and sensed the hot creamy steam.

I could even pull myself up, stuff some pillows behind my back, take the handle from your hands and the mug up to my lips; all without opening my eyes. That was love I would think. And the tea would taste just perfect, whether or not there was too much milk or not enough sugar, or both.

But this morning is the last time I will lie, like a zebra in the jaws of a lion, in these cold covers and this sickening silence. Those beautiful seconds, before I remember who I am, who I was, who you are, who you were and where you are, are getting shorter. I can bear this no longer. I am going to get you back.

Tereasa

Tereasa sits heavily on her soft single bed, staring one by one at a handful of treasured photographs she keeps in an envelope under her mattress. Greying, overweight and in her early fifties, her face is like a hardened cleaning lady's.

There is someone who appears in most of the photos - a bright and soft-skinned girl, with nice teeth and long brown hair. Tereasa can't help but wonder if that might have been her. In one, the girl is standing between a mother and a father, in a purple pinafore and a yellow t-shirt, against the backdrop of a plain rectangular lawn. In another, she has obviously grown into a young woman and sits with a hairdryer by a dressing table, in hotpants and made up with glitter.

Tereasa is aware that the fact she is sitting on her soft single bed, looking through photos, means there must surely have been a time when she was a proper person with a name and a family, or at least a mother and father. But, despite her doctor nudging her to remember bad things that happened, or good ones, there is no one huge event that she can conjure up and say: 'That is when I died inside'. It's not as if she lost her self like you might a leg in a car crash. She had simply faded, like a cup of tea going cold, until she had slipped through her own fingers.

When she looks in the mirror, Tereasa has no idea where she is or how she got there. But occasionally, she does feel what might be a memory. But it's just a little flicker that goes nowhere and doesn't last, like the spark from an empty lighter. It might just be her imagination.

And there's a sickening doubt that none of the people in the photos, not even the soft-skinned girl, are her at all. That she never had a mum or a dad and that the pictures belong to somebody else.

Her doctor is also trying to teach her how to love herself. He asked her to imagine her best friend was unhappy, then phoning this friend up and giving her advice. What advice would she give? What would she want her friend to do to feel better? But Tereasa can't do this because she can't imagine having a friend.

In her sessions with the doctor, Tereasa has recalled a few unpleasant memories that suggest she had a past. There was a man who hit her and locked her in something like a shed. But that is all she can remember and all she wants to remember. She is safe now, on her single bed, in her little room, with a lanyard round her neck reading, 'Tereasa. Resident. Moonbeam Women's Refuge.' Tereasa is a nice enough name to have been given, she thinks. It'll do.

Gaslighter

When Maria met Mike, he was handsome and strong, with a successful career.

He helped her round the house without being asked, doing things she couldn't do on her own. The two-hour train journey from his place to hers meant he had to leave things at her place, for the next time. Razors, changes of clothes, hair gel, toothbrush. Things like that.

When he visited, he would always bring gifts. And when he couldn't, he'd send them in the post. Thoughtful, expensive. So many. Too many.

He could see she was struggling with the bills, so he offered to pay the mortgage. Two incomes were better than one. And the distance between them meant that, before long, he suggested he move in. She was delighted.

But on a Monday morning not long after, she found him lying on her sofa. Stretched out so long she couldn't even sit down. She asked whether he was going to work. He said he didn't have any. She didn't understand.

'You told me you did,' she said.

'I just needed to know if you were a gold-digger,' he replied, shaking his head. 'And now I can see that you are. I see how your eyes have changed when you look at me.'

That night when Maria got home from work there was a gift on her pillow. 'I love you, darling,' read the label.

Over the next few weeks, stubble covered Mike's face and his hair grew long and greasy. Maria wondered why he had left razors in her bathroom and hair gel on her dressing table if he never used them. He lay on her sofa, in the same track suit day after day. She wondered about his changes of clothes hanging in her wardrobe.

When she asked why he didn't look for work, then, he said she knew he was looking; that he'd told her multiple times. But she couldn't recall that conversation. When she said he was being hurtful, he asked why she could only see things from her own point of view.

That night there was a present on her pillow. 'Sorry,' read the label.

When she pleaded with him to leave her alone, he reminded her how lucky she was that someone could put up with her nagging mouth and crooked nose. That night there was a bottle of perfume on her pillow. 'I love you, beautiful,' said a note attached.

When she told him to get out of her house, he said it was his house. When she cried that it wasn't, he showed her the mortgage papers with his name on, not hers. When she yelled she'd tell the police, he smashed her head against the wall and stuffed the paperwork in her mouth.

When she woke, a doctor was peering into her eyes. 'Hello Mandy,' he said.

'Who is Mandy?' she thought. Her name was Maria.

'Welcome back,' he smiled. 'You're in a hospital. You've been sedated for a while.'

'How did I get here?' she asked.

'Your husband brought you in.'

'I don't have a husband.'

'It's OK,' the doctor smiled again. 'Some amnesia's quite common after a head injury like yours. He also left you this present for when you woke up.

poems

The pursuit of happiness

'We hold these truths to be self-evident, that all men are created equal, that they are endowed by their Creator with certain unalienable Rights, that among these are Life, Liberty and the pursuit of Happiness.' From the American Declaration of Independence, 1776

The pursuit of happiness
is the diversion of our time.
We do not see
it's futile
to humankind.
Despite
the trail of misery
we call history
that lies behind.
And while the sorrow
of the moment
lingers on,
we wildly chase
a cheerful place
to depend upon.

The words,
'Oh happiness,
Our being's end and aim!'
Penned by Alexander Pope,
an architect of hope,
are some to blame.
In a tragic world,
his words became
the expectation
of every man born

to tribulation.
And if elation
be compared to liberty
then we're all captive
can't you see?
That you're not bad
for feeling sad,
and next door
they are blue
and troubled too.

The 'I' they don't mention

I have everything in life I ever wanted, yet
I weep with envy at the sight of
lovers on the beach,
and other people's houses.
Adrift on social media,
I have no regard for
my opulent surroundings. Instead,
I'm drenched in lack,
magnetised by tanned Californians
hysterically peddling
cut-price happiness packages.

I have everything in life I ever wanted, yet
my husband makes me angry and
my children make me cry.
Each morning,
God hands me a clean sheet of A4,
to paint whatever colours I choose,
and I choose grey.

I have everything in life I ever wanted, but
I forgot to save up for the 'I'.
It should read,
'Have   everything   in   life   ever   wanted.'

I have a friend. Her name is Fiona.
She was born again
and lives with Jesus.
Her slow, steady breaths calm me down.
I sense no lack behind her words
and there's a smile in her eyes that I trust.

I think the answer may be,
not to have more,
but to believe there's more
than this.

Passionate lies

Clamp your open mouth on mine and wedge my lips apart.

Hold the kiss and please don't break the seal.

Test the vacuum's fast or death might suck us separately towards its gates.

Throw me on the bed and pull my clothes away.

Take me.

Take me there and tell me you will never leave.

Push your chest so hard on mine my breasts splay to the sides.

Crushed we will not breathe but drift in giddy asphyxiation.

Thrust your hips on mine until our bones fragment.

And what re-forms will be a single pelvic bowl, an ivory chariot flying through Cupid's valentine skies.

Slash me with your fingernails and rip the walls away.

Tear out my heart and drink the blood from both your hands.

Smear it on your face and holler 'I will always love you.'

Eat me while I eat you
until all that's left are two locked jaws that wrestle to the death
then seethe into a puff of smoke.

But, too far gone to hold back now,
we come
and all is dark except the stars.

'We   will   always   be   together
We   will   never   ever   part   for   we   are   one.'

But then the light breaks through my eyes and I feel a rip in our seam.

The tremors of our differences rumble on the sheet, and we start to slip apart again like seismic plates.

With every little shift, my lonesomeness returns.

The clamour carries on a while, but,
bone-weary, we let go.
And weep.

Melancholic tears at the human condition, as two eclipses one and, divided,
we fall.

Lost words

Lost words
Begging you to stay
Trying to change your mind
But it's your heart that's left me

Lost words
Falling at your feet
With my tears, shedding
Ink on to the wooden floor

A knock at the door

One day, as I lay dreaming,
a knock knock knock
came knocking at my door.
What a bore!

That pesky tap-tap-tapping
tried to tuck itself in to my bed.
And slide itself into my head.
'What a cheek,' I thought.
'A bore and a cheek.
No more!'

So, I went back to the clouds,
where I'd been flying high.
All fluffy clouds and wings,
and pies in the sky.

But, oh, bang bang bang bang it went,
trying to get into my dream.
I billowed in the heavens thinking,
'What does all this mean?'

'Must I leave my nice warm bubble,
crack it open, watch it break?
Risk what's out there on the shores
of this big black lake?
Let in the light and sigh goodbye?
And never ever learn to fly?'

But 'Oh no no no,' came the answer.
'You can't come in!

What's so urgent, knocker,
that you're making such a din?
I tell you, you get lost, and give me a break.
What's so great, anyhow, about being awake?'

'And I know I'm in no trouble,
so you won't break down the door.
You'll tire of bang bang banging soon,
and leave sometime, for sure.
And I'll stay searching merrily,
my back against the door,
'cos in my dreams are the answers
I've been looking for.'

So, 'Lights, camera, action',
let it roll and let it run.
I watched and learned and dreamt
until the story was done.

So, leave the knocks and rings
and the small earthly things.
Don't lift your lids
if they're not ready,
nor your eyes
if they're too heavy.

Mother lines

Five years before your incarnation, I sensed I was being followed.
I was drawn towards the fractals of femininity,
recurring in my womb.
And of all the women to come after me, you,
in particular, stood out.
A girl, with thicker hair than mine. My daughter.

Five years later, I felt the flutter of your fully fuelled wings,
as you descended from ether to ovary, from ovary to womb.
I thickened my walls around you with blood
and fed you long before you had a mouth.
Your way was paved with love long before you grew a heart.

But I always knew that, one day, you would want to run ahead.
Too fast, like a storm, too wild, like a torrent.
That you wouldn't stay by my side,
as I lolled along in the gentle breeze and
floated with the flow of this river.
That you'd catch your toes and trip,
on the only path you'd ever tread,
surging to the fore,
digging in your heels,
yet finding nothing I hadn't already found.

Because girls these days repeat the mistakes
of the mothers and grandmothers on whose shoulders they stand.
Driven by the immortality of youth,
they care not to look back along the matriline.

Until it's too late.

I always knew that, one day,
I'd become an embarrassment to you.
A mere glance over your shoulder,
my sagging breasts and greying hairline, my limp,
abhorrent reminders.
And that, even though the bricks of your temple
were laid with the cells of my hands,
you'd leave.

But, I have always, also, known that the day will come,
when it is you who'll sense you're being followed.
That, one day, in the mirror,
your every new wrinkle will scream 'I told you so.'
And each white hair will whisper, 'Elder.'
And only then will you look to me to answer
your big questions. But
I'll be standing on the edge of the cliff, by then, ready to jump.
Because every outer Russian doll must crack to reveal its inner.

You didn't listen, my darling. You assumed
my spirit would stay yours once I was dead.
But you got it the wrong way round.
I am here for you while I live.
But after that you're on your own.

England

There once was a country
so fair,
she roused romantic poets,
to promise themselves,
not to women or boys,
but just to her temperate lands.

So dependable was she, that,
yearlong,
she would walk aside
Wordsworth, Shelley, Keats…
lucky men,
her loyalty taken for granted.

For them,
a wildflower was predictable.
It blossomed and died,
just as the English tides, they rose and fell,
and the even-tempered grasslands of the moors
laid down their dusky heather cloaks.

In spring,
they could take off their shirts
then put them back on.
In winter,
their leathers and wools would empower them
to set off and capture a snowflake.

In summer,
they ripped off their clothes, splayed bare,
and absorbed all she had to give.

And in autumn, they lamented,
as the trees shed
and birds flew away.

But, not so,
any longer,
as we wade
with trepidation
through these ever-warmer flooded fields.
And tiptoe
on unsteady rocks,
in hope

not of inspiration,
but salvation.

Alibi

Where do you run when
the peril's
at home? When
his arm is around your daughter?

When he's reading her
a bedtime story and
his hand
awaits your return?

You can run along lanes
lined with flat, locked
doors, cosy
windows casting
gold light upon the
knife-edge pavements.

You can run to the police
who want bruises,
and you have some,
but your daughter loves him,
and she's your only living
blood alibi.

All the others are dead or
across the globe, or a
bus ride away and you're in your
nightdress.

And your friends think

you're mad because he says you are, and
you're out in the dark
in your nightdress.

No such woman
has an alibi. That's why she's
running
on cold nights, hiding
in urine shelters
on tilted benches,
curled around armrests that
cut her in half.

Where do you run when
all you want is to
smell your little
daughter's breath?

You run back
into his arms
again. That's
where you run.

On covid

As I lay fading from C19,
I reached out for some strong green grass to call
my own.
But as I did, the ground beneath me
quivered.
'What's wrong?' I asked her, honestly.
But I knew.
So I climbed onto my knees and knelt upon the
lawn. I stilled,
my body bowing, my fingers pushing,
deep into her infinite skin.
'I know,' I said.

But then each earthly blade rose up and
slashed my palms. My blood
turned the green grass brown.
She drank it,
then she flinched, recoiled.
I tried to jump away,
but her battleground,
beneath my knees,
sucked me down,
and there was no more gravity,
nor light. And I was floating,
kicking the wind,
grasping at blackness for something to hold.
My throat swelled more, my lungs felt crushed
and boiling sweat
dripped from my lip down to my breast.

And then she spoke,

her breath as warm as was my blood.
'Sometimes, children don't listen, and must be punished.'

'But I am listening!' I gasped, finding no air for a voice.
'So, listen!' she said.
And I was drawn back to the ground again,
to air and dew, and sweet, sweet Earth,
beloved home.

'There was a long, long time, before you were born,'
she said,
when you had no eyes,
nor ears, nor flesh,
and all you were was heart.
You were part of the breeze
that blows in the fields
and the scents that waft from the flowers. You were
the light from the sun,
and the glow of the moon
and the twinkling of the stars.
'But then,' she sighed, in a deep and billowing breath,
'you pulled away,
grew eyes to see
and ears to hear
and a mouth to speak and feed.
And with those eyes you saw what you wanted.
And with those ears you chased what you heard.
I let you go.
I let you find that everything you'd ever dreamt of
was there.

I let you gorge on every plant and tree, until
you tired of all their tastes.
I let you lust the meat of animals and
spear them roughly as they grazed upon the
grass.
I let your flesh find other flesh and you bore
children and
formed your clan.
Then when you were fat, I let you chop me
up,
and you said,
"This is my land and not your land,"
and you put fences round that which you
claimed. You said,
"This is my food that grows in my field."
'And I watched
as you richened and your family grew idle.
You sold food for protection and
killed any hungry soul who dared
to trespass on your land.
I watched you learn the tricks of war, and
how to fight,
build hierarchies, and always keep yourself
on top,
and call it class or caste,
for fear of losing
what was never really yours at all.

'But it was when I saw your children,
rise up, leave their schools and
march, in masks
to protect their lungs from your noxious air,
chanting for a future, pleading for a chance,

I had to protect them, as any parent would.
I had to blind you for a while. Restart your
hearts.
I had to save the air and clear the skies,
clean the seas and stop the cars.
I had to pause it all.

'Now, will you help me?' she asked. 'If so, we
have a pact.
You can live if you do exactly as I say.
I'll give you one task a day. And will return
the next to give you another.'

'Of course,' I gasped,
and felt my chest expand
with the blessed breath of life.

'Your first task,' she said,
'is to leave your home to those who need it
more than you.
Don't worry,' she said, 'It will feel good.'
And with that, she was gone.

I once swam, naked

I once swam, naked,
in sea-level seas,
before the waves swelled up
and the rivers burst their banks
before the waters blistered
under our paddling feet
and the shrunken lakes
left nothing for us to drink.

I used to love
to climb the trees
I saw devoured by beetles,
powered by the heat.
I watched as hurricanes
tore out boats and hurled them on
corroding rocks,
so all that was left of the fishing ports
were ghosts
and piles of empty lobster pots and
wild, torn nets,
dissolved in banks of cracking mud.

We used to say that April was the
cruelest month,
illuminating souls of the sad.
How naive we were, as we moaned
that fluffy clouds obscured the sun.
Now, Earth,
her lush, green belt,
just a strike of callous ash,
a body beaten,

black where the fires raged,
blue where they
all drowned at sea.

And as I look upon
this still and rusty soil,
I can't help asking,
Where is God?

I want to know

When my mother
passed away,
I realised
she'd taken with her
memories
of my youth.
Ones I had forgotten.

They may say, 'Hush!
Don't ask.
Best that you forget.
It's for a reason.
Protects you from the pain.'
But,
I don't care.
I
want
to
know.

So,
flicking through the album leaves
of thick black card,
the ones in the attic,
where poses
and say cheeses
cling
with crispy sellotape,
I went in search of
ME.

But, there,
between the faded Polaroids
and oversaturated Kodacolour snaps,
the tatty black and whites
and the dogeared, discoloured prints,
lay a deep,
dark
silence
and a lot
of space.
Space in which
the honest fabric
of my life
had been woven
inconspicuously.
Off camera.

Where the young girl
I once was,
was stored,
in the dark,
for decades.
Her grin,
frozen.
Her golden hair
in locks,
for which,
the key
was lost.

I think
I can see happiness
there in her face.

But how can I know?
She could have been
pretending,
captured,
there on camera.
Quietly plotting
to run away.
Secrets,
hidden,
like rocks
in the pockets
of her pinafore.

I search her eyes.
They are more alive
than mine are now.
'Have we met somewhere,
before?'
I ask her,
feeling
nothing.

She's wearing a swimsuit
and armbands
with sand castles,
buckets and spades,
at her feet.
Behind her
is the English sea
and a bicycle,
with stabilisers,
propped against a wall.

'Can you swim?'
I ask her.
'Do you like the beach?
Is that your bike?
Do you ride?'

But she doesn't speak
and doesn't move.
So I take the album
and shake it.
'Wake up, little me,'
I say,
'and show me!
I'm giving you a second chance!'

And then,
a little whisper comes.
A tiny,
tiny voice.
There,
in her bathing costume,
by her bike,
I feel her shiver.
And as the shiver continues,
down my spine,
she softly says,
'I'll show you, then!
Let's cycle to the beach!'

She is about to ride away,
when 'Stop!' I call to her.
'I can't ride!
Don't even have a bike!'

'Oh, yes you do!' she laughs.
'Go look in the shed.
At the back, on the right.'

So I run,
to the garden's end,
to a shed of abandoned things.
At the back,
submerged by boxes,
is, indeed, a rusty, rough old bike.
I drag it free,
and mount the saddle,
push on a pedal
and the wheels turn.
I *can* ride!

I catch her up and shout.
'Me! Wait. I can't swim!'
'Oh yes you can!'
she says.
'Let's head for the beach.'

I cycle by my friend's house,
to borrow a bathing suit.
'But, you can't swim!'
says my friend.
'Just lend it me anyway,
will you?
Maybe
I can.'

I pedal the bike
to the coast,

and look upon the waves.
I prop the bike against a wall
and put on the bathing suit.
And then
I walk.
Out
to sea.
Through the solid waves,
I push,
my legs
scalded by November cold.
I wade
until I'm hidden in
the freezing wind.

I surrender
to my fate, as
I hear her words,
'Oh yes you can!'
and my feet
loosen on the seabed.
My legs
rise behind me
and my body
lifts
in the waves.
My hands
part the waters and
I move ahead.
I *can* swim!

In that moment,
which is all I have left,

I am so proud
of myself.
I look
towards the shore
and see my mother
watching over me.

'Look, Mama!
No armbands!'
I cry.

Don't stop dreaming

Holiday makers
are fugitives.
They fly and fly
Through polluted skies.
They ride and ride
Through cities' backsides.
Red and yellow adverts
Catch the sides of their eyes.
MacDonald's
Pepsi
'Land of Smiles.'
'Tui. Don't stop dreaming.'

Tired, they need a holiday
but there's nothing to eat or drink.
'You have reached your destination,'
says the pilot, on arrival.
They shuffle along the fuselage
'til a sign reads, 'Finishing line.'

'Prize draw. Tickets here,'
says the hostess with the mostess.

'Congratulations', she tells them,
'You're in fourth position!
Don't stop dreaming, now!'
and hands out tickets saying '4th'.

In the terminal building,
a lady gives out prizes.
Third,

a £1 Lucozade voucher.
Second,
a £2.50 MacDonald's coupon.
And first prize,
£25 credit for 'Tui. Don't stop dreaming.'

Eulogy

If I muttered words
to satisfy your expectations,
I might just draw him down again,
below the dancing stars,
and weigh him to this earth.

Yes, he was my son,
but now he's gone.
He's free,
to be
whatever he'll become.

So, don't look back beloved.
Choose a name to excite your way.
Fly! Fly,
you angel,
to the light.

After parties

We made the effort
Shook our batties
Waved our hands up in the air.
The DJ sweated
Loved ones petted
Pretended they didn't care.

Oh youthful party
Let's be naughty
I'm letting down my hair.
Debauched and dirty
Take your pants off
If you dare.

The sound was deafening
Your hand was grasping
I can't remember you.
You pushed inside me
It was a ball.
That was all.

And though it ended
Before we od'd
And silence filled the air.
My deafness
And depression
Prove that
I was there.

So grape and grain,
Please come again
Let me forget despair.

Let me feel sexy
Let me feel free
Come home with me.

Silence

All that is beheld,
and all that can be known,
where no external thing is there,
to stuff the silence
and fill the space,
like birdsong,
as it rides the air,
or the wind
as it blows,
or a child
as she cries,
are the deepest of our dreams,
rebellious recollections,
colouring the blackness
and padding it with fears.

The longer is the silence
outside the world of form,
the more we gasp in disbelief,
yet spellbound,
at what lies beyond
this world's illusion.
Silence,
is but emptiness,
but silent,
and still.
It is only what it does not say.
Is nothing but the words,
no thing,
and never,
not to be.

It is the lack of outside sound,
of any art external,
painted by another's brush,
a story told by strangers.
Suspense lies
not in Hitchcock films,
nor in the darkened alleys
in the midst of night,
but in our own imaginings,
mustered up from memories,
and fuelled by fear,
where we find that we are
terrified
by ourselves.

Maud or something like that

I don't remember
the colour of her eyes,
the classmate who stole my joy
and taught me to disguise.
I don't even recall
the colour of her hair
that teacher's pet who blanked me
and drove me to despair.
I don't remember
the way she used to dress
that favourite kid who bullied me
from wonder to distress.
I don't even
remember her name
the girl who for my sadness
I'm forever to blame.
I think that schoolgirl's name was Maud
or something here nor there.
She taught me winning was for those
pretending not to care.
One thing I do remember, though,
is deciding to be like that.
From that day on I've been a bitch
So thank you Maud for that.

The leaf

On the axis curls the grass,
The Thames' banks, and Primrose Hill,
Where here upon the middle earth
My birth allies come parallel.

To the north, the west, the south and east,
The one Great Tree's roots bore,
Through earthen skies and just as far
To the Earth's heavenly core.

I *have* to grasp beyond the veil,
for what I know I know,
So fuelled with longing for a home,
And yet be free, I go.

Into the trunk, where damp, sweet soil
Both shrouds and fills my head
A bore of root vines cradle me
As I fall and twist and spread.

And land,
Where dear old Panther waits
To dismember me
Before the gates
To the underworld
Where lost soulparts
Float in flames
Into which I dance
Null and void
In mini-death,
For it's no place

For epithets.

And when I rise
All empty-handed,
Light and kind,
I'm Jane disbanded.

Were a Christian to see,
They'd say that I'd done wrong
That underneath this flattened Earth
only the Devil belongs.
And to know my place
As only Priests,
In the name of Christ,
Can tame such beasts.

But I would say
There is no devil.
Only fear
Of one's own evil.
And I've no more delved
In wizardry
Than were I having
Psychotherapy.

And a fallen leaf dances
To the ground.

Last call

When all around's ablaze
we look
inside.

We ask not 'where do I run?'
but
'to who?'

In birth we are alone
and
once we're dead.

But we try
to die
together.

If there was only time
for one
'I love you'

Who would you call?

In times of crisis
we must choose
who we most love.

The silence of ears

Every man an island is,
within the others' grief,
mouth gagged,
hands bound to his rage.
The silence of ears, feet
scarpering in the other direction,
apologetic eyes, downwards
smiling sighing lips.
Before this time, I knew
the sun would rise
but, now, I'm not so sure, walking
head-high on the golf-course,
down the motorway, kicking stones,
peering for birds.
The skies,
no longer tell of travels,
but hold tiny storms of sorrow,
black inside rainclouds.

The author

Janie Reynolds was born in London in 1963 to a German-Jewish father who escaped Nazi Germany to be adopted by British Quakers, and an English atheist mother with communist sympathies. Before Janie was born, her anthropologist parents lived in the Ugandan jungle studying wild chimpanzees. She won the Faber & Faber 'Hard Lines' short story competition at the age of 19 while training to be a journalist at the London College of Printing. She went on to study psychology and philosophy at Middlesex University, then devoted 20 years to animal welfare campaigns, founding her own non-governmental organisation, People Against Chimpanzee Experiments, which fought for and achieved a ban on the use of great apes in medical research. For the past 20 years she has been a practising osteopath.